RN

Book 1

To Steve – for his love and knowledge of all things Indian.

First published in 2011 in Great Britain by
Barrington Stoke Ltd
18 Walker St, Edinburgh, EH3 7LP

www.barringtonstoke.co.uk

ISBN: 978-1-84299-571-6

Printed in China by Leo

The publisher gratefully acknowledges support from the Scottish Arts Council towards the publication of this title.

Scottish
Arts Council

WHO ARE TRIBE?

ARE THEY HUMANS?

OR ARE THEY ANIMALS?

Tribe are humans *and* animals.

They are super-heroes with special powers.

They can *shape-shift* – change from animals to humans and back again.

THEIR PLAN: to save the world from anyone who tries to destroy it.

Tribe need to find the bad guys – before it's too late.

The Earth is in trouble – and only Tribe have the power to help.

Tribe are helped by TOK – the Tree Of Knowledge.

Tribe can travel all over the world using the roots of trees.

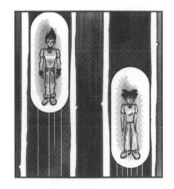

Tribe also have the power to talk to animals – and they can send each other mind-messages, even when they are miles apart.

CAST LIST

Finn

Bruin

Kat

Mo

Talon

Vana

and ...

Kong Kreet!

Contents

Chapter 1
Going West

The branches of the Tree Of Knowledge, TOK, hid a huge tree-house. Inside it was Tribe's Head Quarters.

The Sap Screen flashed red. An alarm!

The Tree Of Knowledge woke up. "Tribe! You are needed."

"What's up?" said Bruin.

Vana looked at the Sap Screen. "Someone needs help," she growled. "In the USA."

"Great!" said Finn. "I've always wanted to go to the USA!"

Vana smiled. "You might get your chance now, Finn. They need our help on an Indian Reservation."

"What's a Reservation?" asked Finn.

"It's land the Indians have been given to live on. It's beautiful and wild," Vana told him.

Kat had been asleep. She woke up and yawned. "So what's the problem?"

"A man called Kong Kreet wants to build a road to go right through the Reservation," snarled Vana.

"Why?" said Finn, with a frown.

"Because it will make him rich. He makes new towns. The road will link his towns, so he can sell more houses. He knows it's against the law but he doesn't care. He thinks no one can stop him," said Vana.

"We'll make him think again," hissed Kat. "Think of all the terrible fumes from a busy road like that ..."

"It will harm the trees and frighten all the animals away," whispered Mo.

"Why don't the Indians stop him?" asked Finn.

"They tried but Kong Kreet cheated them," said Vana. "We're the Indians' last hope. He has to be stopped."

"You're right, sis," said Talon. "Let's get over there."

"Tribe to the rescue!" roared Bruin.

Tribe jumped into the nearest tree trunk and sped along the tree root system. The root system took them anywhere in the world that had trees.

By the time Tribe got to the Reservation, night had fallen. Vana gazed up at the moon.

"I'll go for a run and find out what the other wolves know about Kong Kreet's plans. I'll send a mind-message to tell you what I find out."

They could all send mind-messages to each other – it was like talking without words. It was one of their special gifts – but they had others, too.

Vana morphed into a wolf and let out a long, loud howl.

"I'll have a look round, too," said Kat, changing into her cat form. It was time to prowl.

"Oh, no! Look at that!" squeaked Mo.

The others looked where Mo was pointing. Huge tractors and diggers were lined up in a row, waiting to rip up the land.

"Grr!" said Bruin. "It looks like they're going to start digging. How can we stop Kong Kreet?"

"I've got an idea!" said Vana. "We'll make Kong Kreet and his men think the machines are haunted! We'll make them believe that the spirits of the Indians are after them!"

Chapter 2
Tribe on the Warpath

Talon flew into the sky to keep watch. His eagle eyes could see for miles. He would warn the others when Kong Kreet and his men were on their way back to start digging the road.

"This is a job for you, Mo," said Vana. "Be quick – we don't have much time."

"I'll do my best," squeaked Mo. She morphed into a mouse and scampered off.

First she went to the big digger and nibbled through the cables in the driver's cab. Then she ran over to the other machines and nibbled and nibbled and nibbled.

Talon swooped down to warn them that Kong Kreet and his men were on their way. Mo hid in the tall grass and waited.

Kong Kreet climbed into the big digger and tried to turn it on. It wouldn't start.

"This darn digger won't start," he said. "We'll have to use a tractor instead."

"The tractors are all bust, too, boss," said another man. "Something has chewed through the wires."

Kong Kreet was very angry. All the machines were broken.

"Get new ones, then!" he yelled.

That night, Mo crept back and nibbled through even more cables and wires.

"It's a good thing I have strong teeth," she squeaked.

"Me, too," said Bruin. He had used his huge teeth and claws to rip the tractor's heavy tyres.

****

In the morning all that Kong Kreet and his workers found were the tracks of a big bear and of a little mouse – and lots of broken machines.

"Look at these mouse tracks! Look at these bear tracks! It's the Indians, boss," said one man. "They're shape-shifters – their spirits can turn into any animal!"

"That's impossible!" shouted Kong Kreet. "I don't believe in spirits. I'm going to build this road – and no one will stop me!"

"Yes, we will!" squeaked Mo.

You don't have to be big to be the best.

Chapter 3
Kong Kreet Fights Back

There was a dust cloud far off on the horizon. It was getting bigger and bigger and darker and darker. Something was coming. Something big.

"What is it?" squeaked Mo.

Talon flew up high to have a look, then swooped back down.

"They've got a tank!" he said. "A great big tank! Oh, no!"

"That doesn't matter to me," said Mo. "I can still creep inside and chew through the cables. It's just like playing hide and squeak!"

Mo morphed into her mouse form and scampered off.

"*Tank* goodness for Mo!" growled Bruin who was hiding behind a spiky cactus with Talon.

"I thought I heard a mouse squeak," said one of the men.

"What do you want me to do about it?" yelled Kong Kreet. "Oil it?"

Kong Kreet was very angry. First his diggers wouldn't work. Then his tractors wouldn't work – and now his tank was broken, too! He didn't understand what was going on.

"This place is haunted, boss!" snivelled one of his men. "I'm getting out of here."

"You stay right there!" yelled Kong Kreet. "We'll use spades if we have to!"

The men began to dig the road by hand, but they were not happy. It was hot, hard work.

"Now we can really frighten them," growled Bruin. "You go first, Vana."

Vana morphed into a wolf. She stood on the top of a small hill, lifted her head and howled.

"What's that?" shouted the men.

"It's just a wolf!" yelled Kong Kreet.

Vana's howl called all the other wolves. They came running. Hundreds of wolves made a circle round Kong Kreet and his men. The wolves glared at them with their yellow eyes and licked their lips.

"Let's get out of here, boss!" said one of the men.

"Your turn, Talon," growled Bruin.

Talon morphed into his eagle form and flew high into the air. He let out a mighty screech and swooped down on the men. They dived onto their hands and knees and shook like jellies.

"Now it's my turn," said Bruin. He morphed into a bear.

"ROAAAAAAR!" said Bruin. He stood on his back legs, showing his huge teeth and long claws.

"Help! It's the spirits of the Indians!" said the men.

They ran away, falling over each other in a panic as they tried to escape from bears and wolves and eagles. The wild-life was too wild for them.

"Now for my last trick!" growled Bruin.

"I'll make Kong Kreet vanish!"

Chapter 4
Bruin Rides Again

Mo was ready to go. She held a thin bit of wire in her mouth as she scampered over to the big digger. Using her tiny mouse paws, she tied the wire around the big digger's cables so it wasn't broken any more.

She squeaked loudly so that Bruin's

sharp bear ears would hear her. He

lumbered over to the digger and climbed
into the driver's seat.

"Kong Kreet won't be able to *bear* it
when he sees this!" he grinned to himself.

The digger roared into life – and charged
at the evil Kong Kreet.

Kong Kreet couldn't believe his eyes. He
rubbed his eyes and shook his head – yes, it
really was a big brown bear driving a
digger!

The digger charged at him with Bruin at
the controls.

Kong Kreet ran. He fell over, ripping his smart clothes and getting covered in dust.

"Ho, ho, ho!" laughed Bruin. "What time is it when a bear is charging at you in a digger truck? Time to run!"

Bruin scooped Kong Kreet into the digger's bucket. "I'm being kidnapped by Yogi Bear!" he yelled.

Suddenly Bruin saw something that made him grin even more – a huge cactus. He drove up to it and dumped the evil Kong Kreet right on top of the prickly plant.

"Ow! Ow! Ow!" yelled Kong Kreet.

"Now you get the *point*!" growled Bruin. "And don't come back!"

Kong Kreet had had enough. He ran away, holding his sore bottom.

Tribe had won. They stood together as the dust settled. The sun began to set and the sand glowed orange and red.

"Well," squeaked Mo, "I think we got to the *bottom* of that problem!"

Tribe went home, happy that they had done a good job. As the day turned to darkness the spirits of the Indians rose from the ground.

"Thank you, brothers," they said. "Thank you, sisters."

NEW ROADS, NO JOKE

Do we need more roads?

Every time there is a new road, you get more traffic. This is because if there are new, fast roads people want to drive more. America has more roads than any other country in the world: six-and-a-half million miles of road. That many roads could go round the world 270 times!

The people who make these roads should spend years finding out if they will do any harm to the environment. They have to think about what animal habitats could be destroyed and if pollution from cars could be a problem. But some people, like Kong Kreet, don't care about the environment.

Instead of always going by car, people could take the train or bus or walk or go by bike.

If you want to find out more, go to www.sustrans.org.uk.

MO – MOUSE GIRL

SHE IS QUIET AND SHY BUT
LOYAL TO HER FRIENDS. SHE'S
LIKE THE GLUE THAT KEEPS THE
GANG TOGETHER.

SPECIAL SKILL: can jump long

distances and can move like a shadow

in fluffy slippers.

LOVES: cheese, chocolate buttons,

small spaces.

HATES: mousetraps, rats, rat poison.

MOST LIKELY TO SAY: "Er ... um ...

I've got an idea."

BIGGEST SECRET: she's frightened of

Kat.

TRIBE TALK!

To: Mo

From: Kerry

Subject: Cycling to School

Dear Mo,

I'd like to cycle to school but my

mum says it's quicker to take the car.

What can I do?

Kerry

To:	Kerry
From:	Mo
Subject:	Re: Cycling to School

Dear Kerry,

Tell her there are more traffic jams on school days. Petrol is very expensive.

Why not cycle to school with a friend – but don't forget to wear your cycle helmet. It'll be fun and you'll get fit.

Squeak to you later,

Mo

FYI: MiCE

One mouse but two mice!

 • The smallest breed of mouse weighs just 7g.

• Cheese isn't very good for mice! It gives them tummy upsets.

 • House mice walk and run on all fours, but eat sitting on their back legs.

 • A pet mouse can live up to 3 years, but in the wild most mice only live for 4 months.

 • Mice can't vomit!

JOKE OF THE DAY

MO: What does a mouse have that no other animal has?

KAT: I don't know...

MO: Baby mice!

CHECK OUT THE REST OF
THE TRIBE BOOKS!

For more info check out our website:
www.barringtonstoke.co.uk